Polly
Pomegranate

Delia Damson

B
B

Alice Apple

Peter
Potato

Grace Grape

Wee Willie
Water Melon

The Garden Gang
Stories and pictures by Jayne Fisher

Other Garden Gang stories

Series 793

Peter Potato

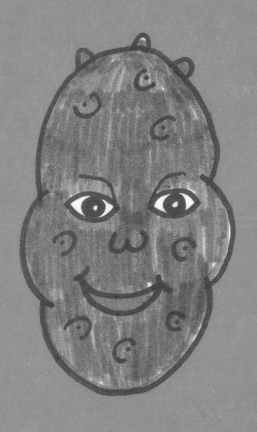

Ladybird Books Loughborough

Peter Potato
was pretty good
at making and
mending things.
He had endless patience
and never tired of
inventing new gadgets
to make life easier
for the Garden Gang.
They brought all their
broken tools to him
and he mended them
in no time at all.

4

A brand new tool shed
arrived in the garden
one morning.
It was brought
on the back of
a huge red lorry
which had
driven carefully
into the yard at
the back of the house.
Two strong men
unloaded it,
and Mr Rake proudly
inspected his new shed.

MAN 1

Mr Rake spent
all that day emptying
the old tool shed
and arranging his
tools neatly
in the new one.
By evening,
all that was left
in the old shed
was a broken
lawn mower,
four wheels from
an old pram
and one or two logs.

Peter Potato had been
watching Mr Rake
all day, and
as he had watched
he had made
a most wonderful plan.
He knew he would
need some help
if his idea was to work,
so he gathered
the Garden Gang together
and told each of them
how they could help.

As soon as it was dark
they all started work.
First the broken
lawn mower
was brought from
the old shed,
then the four
pram wheels,
then the logs,
and they were
all packed into
Peter's back yard.
Finally, the shed itself
was carefully
taken to pieces
and the wood and glass
stored in Peter's yard
with the other things.

13

Days went by and
all that could be heard
from Peter Potato's shed
was banging, clanging
and hammering.
Sometimes dust
could be seen
coming from
the shed windows
but always there was
the gruff voice of Peter
singing as he worked.
The Garden Gang
had been asked
to stay out of the shed.

15

By the end of July,
Peter's shed was
beginning to bulge
at the sides.
In fact you could say
that it was bursting
at the seams.
But still Peter
kept his secret.
"Give me two
more weeks," he said,
"and the job will be
finished."

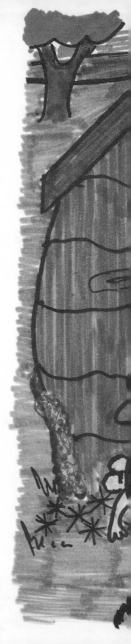

It was early in August
when the banging,
clanging and hammering
finally stopped.
The Garden Gang
looked on excitedly
as the door opened and
Peter Potato came out
into the evening sunshine.
Although he looked
tired and grubby
he had a very contented
smile on his face.
"It's finished," he said.

"Can we see,
can we see?"
called out
the younger fruit
and vegetables.
But Peter only smiled
and said, "Be here
tomorrow evening
at half past six.
Wear something warm
because the evenings
are growing cooler."
With that,
he locked the shed door
and went home to bed.

20

21

At six thirty
next evening,
the Garden Gang
waited outside
Peter's shed door.
Peter opened the door
and went in.
There was
a clicking sound,
then a chugging,
and out of the shed
Peter Potato drove the
most beautiful engine
ever seen,
and it was pulling
two brightly coloured
coaches.

The coaches were
soon filled with
happy, chattering people
and away they went
for the first of many
nightly rides.
How they all
admired Peter
for his skill
which brought
so much pleasure.
Mr Rake never did
find out
what had happened
to his old garden shed.
But...

we know
don't we!

Alice Apple

Alice Apple was always
full of fun and merriment.
She could swing
through the apple trees
as nimbly as a monkey
and her tinkling,
infectious laughter
could be heard
all over the garden.
''There goes Alice,''
the Garden Gang
would say, as they
went about their work.
And they would laugh too.

29

Alice's laughter
attracted many visitors
to the garden,
especially birds.
Her joyous sound
made them want to sing,
and this they did.
The friendly,
intelligent robin,
the familiar blackbird
and thrush,
the chattering swallow
and chaffinch,
all contributed to
the rich, sweet song.

31

One day, it had been
particularly warm
and Alice Apple
had been singing
particularly long and loud.
Miss Penelope Strawberry
had joined in the song.
She loved the Summer
and although most of
the Garden Gang
felt hot and sticky
with the heat,
Penelope remained
as cool and fresh
as a daisy.

The Garden Gang
had been working
very hard.
The butterflies had been
particularly busy,
and all in all,
they were feeling
rather tired
and longing for the day
to come to a close.

Evening came at last
and with it,
a cool, gentle breeze
which wafted
the heavenly scent
of apple blossom
down from Alice's tree
in the sleepy garden.
Colin Cucumber was
so tired that he
had climbed early
into his hammock.
And other small creatures
soon tumbled drowsily
into their little beds.
The birds became silent.
All was still.

Suddenly, there was
a faint humming
in the distance.
Soon the humming
became a tremendously
loud droning
and poor Alice
found herself
surrounded by noisy,
swarming bees.
Soon they settled
on the end of the branch
and went to sleep.
But Alice could not sleep.
She sat wide-eyed
all through the night,
not daring to move.

It was much later
next day,
when everyone
in the garden
suddenly sensed
that something
was wrong.
What could it be?
Everything looked
the same.
But where was
the laughter?
Where was the song?
Where was Alice?
Everything was so quiet.

41

As they all hurried
over to the apple tree,
there was much confusion.
Tim Tomato
scratched his nose
on a bramble thorn.
Someone stamped on
Colin Cucumber's toe
and Peter Potato
fell over a fat toad
who was catching flies
in the undergrowth.

43

They arrived at the tree
and all peered up
through the pink blossoms.
Alice Apple was
perched on the end of
a long bough, terrified,
hardly daring to breath,
let alone laugh and sing.
There above her
hung a swarm of bees
which were busily
moving over each other
and humming softly.
The Garden Gang
were horrified.
What could they do
to help her?

Before anyone
could decide
what to do,
the Queen Bee
flew over to Alice
and looked crossly
into her eyes.
"Alice Apple," she said,
"why don't you laugh?
Why don't you sing?
We have a great deal
of honey to make
this year.
Your merry sounds
help us to work.
Please laugh,
please sing."

Alice's frightened eyes
gradually began to smile
and then she broke into
peals of joyous sound.
The birds began to sing.
The Garden Gang
went about their tasks
and the bees
busily collected honey.
Everyone was happy
as the beautiful garden
once again rang with...

Alice's merry laughter!

Paul Pumpkin

Bertie Brussels Sprout

Mark Marrow

Gertrude
Gooseberry

Tim Tomato

Patrick Pear

Avril Apricot